What's Michael?

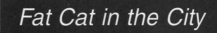

Fat Cat in the City

Story and Art:
Makoto Kobayashi

Translation:
**Dana Lewis, Lea Hernandez,
& Toren Smith**

Lettering and Retouch:
**Amador Cisneros &
Digital Chameleon**

Dark Horse Comics, Inc.®

publisher
Mike Richardson

series editors
Tim Ervin-Gore and Mike Hansen

series executive editor
Toren Smith for **Studio Proteus**

collection editor
Chris Warner

designer and art director
Mark Cox

English-language version produced by
Studio Proteus and
Dark Horse Comics, Inc.

What's Michael? Vol. VII: Fat Cat in the City

This volume collects What's Michael? stories from
issues sixteen through twenty-three of the Dark
Horse comic-book series Super Manga Blast!

The artwork of this volume has been produced
as a mirror-image of the original Japanese
edition to conform to English-language standards.

Published by
Dark Horse Comics, Inc.
10956 SE Main Street
Milwaukie, OR 97222

www.darkhorse.com

To find a comics shop in your area, call the
Comic Shop Locator Service toll-free at
1-888-266-4226

First edition: February 2003
ISBN: 1-56971-914-4

10 9 8 7 6 5 4 3 2 1

Printed in Canada

MY KITTY IS SO *ADORABLE!*

I COULDN'T LIVE WITHOUT HER!

SINGER *MAIKO MIZUGI*

IT DRIVES MY NEIGHBORS *NUTS,* BUT I EVEN FEED THE LOCAL *STRAYS!*

HEH EH HEH

AUTHOR *MINORU SUGU*

I JUST *LOVE* MY KITTIES!

THEY'RE LIKE MY *BABIES!*

ACTRESS *AIKO ISHIKAWA*

IT'S SO WONDERFUL TO SEE THAT YOU ALL LOVE YOUR CATS *VERY MUCH!*

THANKS FOR SHARING WITH OUR VIEWERS THIS EVENING ON--

THE AWFUL TRUTH

--"MAN'S *REAL BEST FRIEND!*" NOW, LET'S HAVE A BIG *PAW* FOR OUR THREE *CAT-CRAZIEST* GUESTS *EVER!*

SEE YOU *NEXT WEEK,* CAT LOVERS!

♪ BYE-BYEEE! ♪

3

4

I... I DON'T OWN A CAT.

B-BUT, MAIKO! THERE WAS A PICTURE OF YOU HUGGING YOUR CHINCHILLA IN PEOPLE!

"She's my love muffin!"

I...I BORROWED HER FROM A FRIEND!

WAS EVERYTHING YOU SAID ON THE SHOW A LIE?!

-SOB!- I'M SORRY! I LIKE CATS, I REALLY DO!!

JUST NOT OWNING THEM!

DON'T CRY, MAIKO. AT LEAST YOU'VE NEVER, SAY...

...ABAN-DONED A CAT!

LIKE I DID! AND SHE WAS PREGNANT, TOO.

HEH EH HEH

MR. SUGU, *NOOOO!* THAT CAN'T BE TRUE! YOU WROTE *LITTLE LIONS IN THE HOUSE* ALL ABOUT YOUR CATS! IT WAS A *BEST-SELLER!*

YOU DON'T *UNDERSTAND!* I...I WAS SO DAMN *POOR* BACK THEN!

THE LANDLORD TOLD ME TO GET RID OF HER OR GET *EVICTED!!*

SO I PUT MY DARLING *HANAKO* IN A CARDBOARD BOX, AND LEFT HER IN A PARK THIRTY MILES AWAY...

IN MY HEART, I'VE BEGGED HANAKO FOR FORGIVENESS A *MILLION TIMES*...BUT THE MEMORY OF HER SAD, LONELY EYES *TORTURES* ME *STILL!*

HANAKO, *FORGIVE MEEE!*

WAHH! AHH! WAHH!

MR. SUGU, I'D WANT TO *DIE* IF I DID THAT!

HOW COULD YOU *BEAR* THE GUILT?

WELL...

A MONTH *LATER*...

SHE CAME HOME! HANAKO CAME HOME!!

AH?! ♥

WONDER-FUL! A HAPPY ENDING!

YOU MUST HAVE BEEN OVERJOYED!

I WAS! I *WAS!* I CRIED LIKE A *LITTLE BOY,* AND I HUGGED AND KISSED HANAKO OVER AND OVER!

≥SNIFF!≤ AND THEN ...?

THEN...

THEN I... I...

I DUMPED HER *FIFTY MILES* AWAY!

WAHHH!

OH, MR. SUGU, *PLEASE* DON'T CRY.

THAT'S *NOTHING* COMPARED TO WHAT I'VE DONE!

EH ...?!

....?

TO TELL THE TRUTH--

--I *RAN OVER* A CAT ON MY WAY HERE!

AIKO! *NOOOO!* SAY IT ISN'T *SO!*

WHAT THE *HELL* WAS I *SUPPOSED* TO DO?!

THE DUMB CAT JUST... JUST *THREW* ITSELF IN FRONT OF MY CAR!

I *SLAMMED* ON THE BRAKES, BUT *BLAMMO!*

WAAAH!

THEY'LL ALL PAY FOR THIS!

THE END

8

FAMILY

MICHAEL

-≥SIGHH≤-

WHY ARE YOU SLEEPING **THERE**, SILLY?

WE MADE YOU A NICE LITTLE HOUSE TO REST IN. COME ON OUT.

MICHAEL COULDN'T **HELP** IT.

9

.....
.....

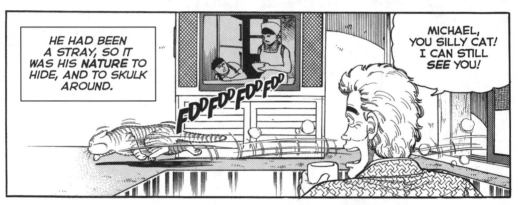

HE HAD BEEN A STRAY, SO IT WAS HIS **NATURE** TO HIDE, AND TO SKULK AROUND.

FOO FOO FOO FOO

MICHAEL, YOU SILLY CAT! I CAN STILL **SEE** YOU!

YOO-HOO! MICHAELLL!

SUPPER-TIME!

COME ON, SWEETIE! DON'T BE SHY.

COME AND EAT.

AND HE WAS FINALLY READY TO BE FRIENDS WITH HIS HUMANS...

AS HUMILIATING AS THAT WAS...

MROW!

AWW! ♥

NYOW R!

KRNCH

12

THE END

14

THIS GUY JUST
FOUND A TWENTY ON
THE SIDEWALK.

HN?

ACTUALLY, MICHAEL HERE IS *INDEED* MAKING FUN OF MR. KOBAYASHI.

BUT FORGET ABOUT THE FACT THAT MICHAEL'S ARTIST HAS BEEN *MOCKED* AND *HUMILIATED* UNMERCIFULLY FOR THIS ENTIRE EPISODE! REMEMBER THAT *PREGNANT* LADY...? WELL, THIS WAS THE FIRST DAY MICHAEL CAME "FACE TO TUMMY" WITH WHAT WAS SOON TO BE HIS *DEADLIEST* RIVAL-- A *HUMAN BABY!*

REVENGE IS SWEET!

THE END

20

23

....!
....!

P-PLEASE, MIKE ....!

HOP DOWN!

I DON'T WANT YOU TO FALL!

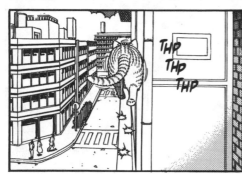

THP THP THP

WAHHG! DON'T RUN!!

SKR CH SKR CH

YEEK! DON'T SCRATCH! KEEP ALL YOUR FEET ON THE RAILING!

WHSSSSH

MMMIIIIKE!

25

MICHAELLL!!! YOU CAN'T GET THAT STUPID BIRD! YOU'RE JUST GONNA *FALL!*

WSSSH

NYOWRR!

NOOOO!!

COME ON!! YOU DIDN'T REALLY THINK MICHAEL WAS GOING TO *SPLAT* HIMSELF OVER A DUMB OLD *SPARROW,* DID YOU?

MEW?

"MEWW" *MY BUTT!* I WANT TO THROW YOU OFF *MYSELF,* NOW!

SADLY, SOME PEOPLE JUST DON'T APPRECIATE A CAT'S SENSE OF HUMOR.

THE END

26

MICHAEL'S BABY SISTER

GOOO...

GMMM!

THIS IS *TAMAMI*-- MICHAEL'S MOST FEARSOME... *ENEMY?!*

MICHAEL, POPO, COME MEET *TAMAMI*...

...YOUR NEW *LITTLE* SISTER!

....? ...?

....!

27

SHE... SHE HAS *NO MERCY!!*

OKAY, THEN--WE HAVE NO CHOICE! IT'S TIME FOR THE *"DINNERTIME CIRCLE AND YOWL"* ATTACK!!

RIGHT!

YOWRR!

MOWR!

NAYOWR!

WAAAAHH! AH AH AWWWHN!

....!

...!

WAH! WAH! WAAHHHN!

SHHH... SHHH...

MY SWEET TAMAMI-AMI IS *HUNGWY,* ISN'T SHE?

WUW- AHHHHNNN!

W-*WOW!* OUR *"DOUBLE DINNERTIME CIRCLE AND YOWL"* ATTACK *BACKFIRED!*

POPO... W-WE'VE *LOST...*

WE DID OUR BEST TRICKS, OUR SNEAKIEST ATTACKS...

YES... AND THE BABY DEFEATED THEM *ALL!*

THEN IT'S TIME TO OFFER OUR TERMS OF *SURRENDER!*

RIGHT!

HMM
...?

....
....

AND SO *MICHAEL* AND *POPO* SURRENDERED TO TAMAMI.

AND WHILE PERHAPS THESE WEREN'T THE MOST *PRACTICAL* BABY GIFTS--IT'S THE *THOUGHT* THAT COUNTS!

THE END

VROOOM

HOOONK

WELCOME TO... THE BIG CITY!

MICHAEL: FAT CAT IN THE CITY

SNIF
SNIFF

QUIET. *RIGHT*. JUST LIKE IT *SHOULD* BE!

MIKE'S WORK DAY ALWAYS BEGINS WITH PATROLLING HIS *TURF.*

WOO, THAT TAKES IT OUTTA ME--TIME FOR *BREAKFAST!*

HMM... HERE?

NOODLES
SOBA/UDON

NOPE... CLOSED.

TUNA?! *HERE* WE GO!

TODAY'S SPECIAL: TUNA STEAK

RESTAURANT

HEY, LOUIE! LOOK WHO IT IS!

I HAVEN'T SEEN YOU IN *FOREVER*, "LUCKY"...!

GOT SOMETHIN' *SPECIAL* FOR YA! IT'S *TUNA* DAY!

MIKE WEARS *MANY HATS* IN HIS LINE OF WORK. AT THIS RESTAURANT, HE'S KNOWN AS "LUCKY." NEXT DOOR, HE'S "STRIPES."

MMM, TUNA! ♥ ALWAYS HITS THE *SPOT!*

SKTCH SKTCH

NO STANDING IN LINE FOR MICHAEL! THERE'S ALWAYS A HANDY SPOT WHEN HE NEEDS TO GO!

TIME FOR A *POWER NAP!*

phew! WHAT A MORNING ...I'M *BEAT!*

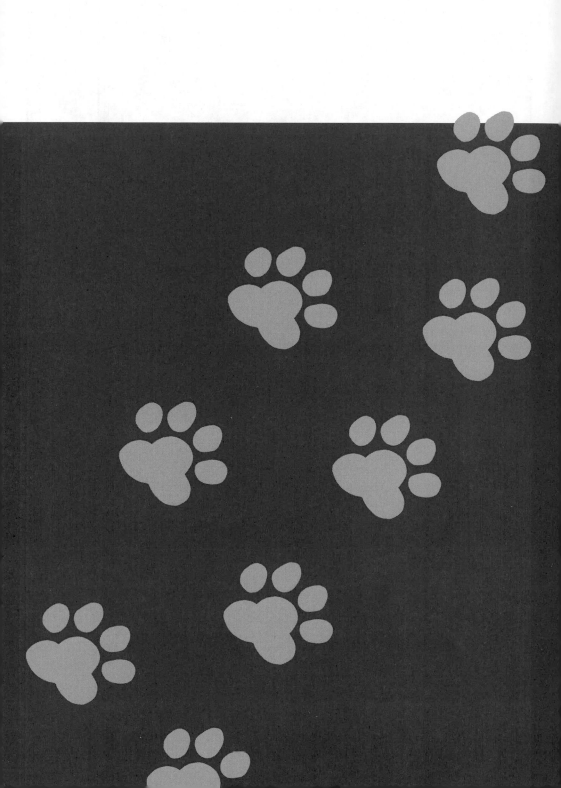

POPO'S BLIND DATE

THIS IS **MISS POPO!**

SHE HAS A MASTER'S DEGREE FROM **MEOWMEOW UNIVERSITY** IN **HOME ECONOMICS** AND WORKS AT "MISS KITTY'S DAYCARE"...!

H-HELLO.

SO NICE TO MEET YOU.

AND THIS FINE FELLOW...

...IS **MISTER BEAR**, A GRADUATE OF **BOWWOW UNIVERSITY**. HE'S **CHOWCHOW TRADING COMPANY'S** ACCOUNTS RECEIVABLE MANAGER!

YUP, THAT'S ME!

PLEASED T' MEETCHA!

40

U—UP A TREE...?

UH...AH CAN'T *DO* THAT.

AH CAN'T EVEN CLIMB A *FOOT* UP A TREE.

ACK!

S... SORRY.

M—ME TOO.

B-BUT, YUH KNOW, AH'M GREAT AT PROTECTIN' MAH PEOPLE! 'CEPT FOR THE TIME AH *SCREWED UP* AND LET A *BURGLAR* IN!

I GOT BEAT *REAL* GOOD FOR THAT!

AH'M SUCH A DOPE, SOMETIMES!

heh ha ha eh...

OH MY GOD...

THERE MUST BE SOMETHIN' *YER* GOOD AT, MISS POPO!

WELL...

THERE *IS*.

WHAT I'M *BEST* AT IS...

...STEALING FOOD! ♥

THERE'S NOT A SALMON STEAK I CAN'T *SNEAK OFF THE COUNTER!* EVERYONE SAYS I'M THE *FASTEST* THEY'VE SEEN!

S-STEALING ...?!

GOSH...HOW 'BOUT THAT...

I DO SHARE...

SAY, MISTER BEAR! W-WHAT... um...

WHAT KIND OF *FAMILY* WOULD YOU LIKE?

GOLLY...!

I WANT LOTSA' PUPS TA *CHASE RABBITS* WITH!

AND WE'D LIVE IN A... A...*BIG OL' MEADOW!*

ULP...!

SO WHAT KINDA' FAMILY WOULD *YEW* LIKE, MISS POPO?

WELL... I *THINK*...

I'D LIKE *LOTS* OF KITTENS THAT LOOK JUST LIKE *ME*!

AND WE'D LIVE IN A CUTE LITTLE *BASKET*!

GUH...!

AH...AH SEE...

TH...THANK YOU.

....
....

....
....

LOVE ISN'T BLIND... BUT APPARENTLY THE MATCHMAKER *IS*.

THE END

THE TRIALS OF CAT OWNERSHIP

IT WAS A BEAUTIFUL, FINE DAY. THE YOUNG CAT OWNER THOUGHT SHE'D TAKE HER CAT MICHAEL TO THE NEIGHBORHOOD PARK.

AT FIRST, MICHAEL WAS *FREAKED OUT.*

BUT HE SOON *ADJUSTED* TO HIS NEW ENVIRONMENT, AND BEGAN TO PLAY.

MROW!

HA HA HA! DON'T GO *TOO* FAR, MICHAEL!

46

THE END

RICHARD KIMBLY THE *FUGITIVE!!* (PROFESSION, *VETERINARIAN.*)

FALSELY ACCUSED OF A *CRIME* HE DID NOT COMMIT, *WRONGLY* SENTENCED TO *DEATH* FOR MURDERING HIS OWN *BELOVED WIFE* (AND CERTAIN OTHER NAUGHTY BEHAVIORS), HE ESCAPED BY THE *SKIN* OF HIS *TEETH* FROM A *TRAIN WRECK* EN ROUTE TO THE *PENITENTIARY!*

A PERPETUAL *FUGITIVE* FROM THE *CEASELESS PURSUIT* OF THE RELENTLESS *LT. GERARDLY!*

sutro baths cosmetics

ENDLESSLY SEEKING THE *BUCK-TOOTHED MAN,* LAST SEEN *FLEEING* THE SCENE OF THE *CRIME!*

RICHARD KIMBLY! HIS LIFE AS AN INNOCENT *FUGITIVE* CONTINUES!

SAN FRANCISCO KARAOKE FEST!

HM ...?

AH ONLY DRUNK MYTHELF TH~~ICK ♪

BECUTH A' YOU~UU, BAH-BY! ♪ ♪

AH ...?

HEY! YOU!!

HAH ...?

IT'S YOU, BUCK-TOOTHED MAN!

I'VE FOUND YOU AT LAST!!

STOP!!

AW, RATSTH!

I CAN'T *ABANDON* AN *INJURED* CAT!!

.....! .....!

I AM A *VET!* LEAVE THIS TO *ME!!*

OH, THANK *GOD!!* PLEASE *HELP!*

GAD! HE HAS NO *PULSE!*

I MUST PERFORM *CAT CPR!*

DON'T *WORRY--* HE CAN BE *SAVED!*

BUT GET A TAXI, *IMMED-IATELY!*

Y-YES, *SIR!!*

KURIHARI VETERINARY

DOGS - CATS - ETC.

1434 IRVING ST.

HE SHOULD BE ALL RIGHT.

THANKS TO YOUR PROMPT, *SKILLFUL* INTERVENTION, SIR!

THANK *GOD!* MY DEAR *MICHAEL!*

I MUST ASK... HAVE YOU *EXPERIENCE* IN THE *VETERINARY SCIENCES?*

ER... ....

N-NO. NONE.

AND NOW, I MUST *GO...*

WHAT ?!

PLEASE DON'T LEAVE YET!

CAN'T I AT LEAST BUY YOU DINNER?!

THANK YOU...

BUT MY TIME IS SHORT.

HM... ...

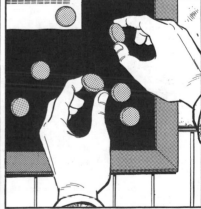

55

THESE MAGNETS ARE QUITE POWERFUL...

SNAP!

....?

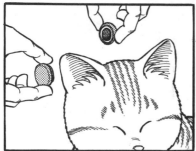

SNOP!

HEH... CHECK IT OUT!! HEE HEE HEE!

WAA HA HA HA HA!!

RICHARD KIMBLY FUGITIVE!

WILL HIS DAY OF FREEDOM EVER COME ...?!

THE END

56

GRANDMA

TODAY'S A SPECIAL DAY FOR KIMIKO-- FOR THE FIRST TIME, HER GRANDMOTHER WAS VISITING FROM THE COUNTRY.

JUST SET YOURSELF DOWN AND RELAX! I'LL MAKE SOME TEA.

THANKEE, HONEY. MY OLD BONES ARE ACHING!

HMN ....?

HMN ....?

HIS NAME'S *MICHAEL*, GRANNY.

ISN'T HE *CUTE?!*

....
....

....
....

MEEYOWR?

....
....

LORD A' *MERCY*... I DON'T KNOW *WHAT'S* COME OVER CATS THESE DAYS.

....!

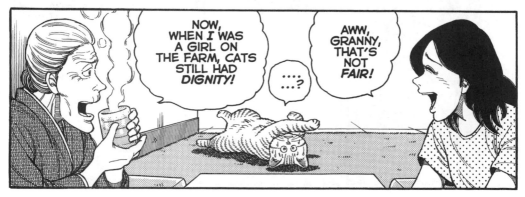

NOW, WHEN *I* WAS A GIRL ON THE FARM, CATS STILL HAD *DIGNITY!*

....?

AWW, GRANNY, THAT'S NOT *FAIR!*

58

IT *HAIN'T*? THEN *TELL* ME--

--HOW MANY *RATS* DOES THIS HERE CRITTER *CATCH* IN A DAY?

HMPH!

AW, *GRANNY*! I'M SURE IF MICHAEL EVER HAD THE CHANCE, HE'D BE *GREAT* AT CATCHING RATS!

RATS...?! COME ON, GRANNY!

WE'RE IN A MODERN *CONCRETE* APARTMENT BUILDING. WE DON'T *HAVE* RATS!

I CAN'T ABIDE *EXCUSES*, YOUNG LADY!

I'LL HAVE YOU KNOW I'M *VERY PARTICULAR* ABOUT CATS!!

HMN ...?

DAG *NABBIT!* MOVE YER *TAIL*, CAT!

GO *CATCH* THAT THERE BIRD!!

EEK! GRANDMA, *NO!* HE COULD FALL OFF THE *BALCONY!*

HMPH! DOWNRIGHT *PATHETIC!*

CAIN'T EVEN CATCH A *SPARROW!*

SKTT *SKTT*

YOWRRR!

ENOUGH!

I CAIN'T *TAKE* NO MORE!

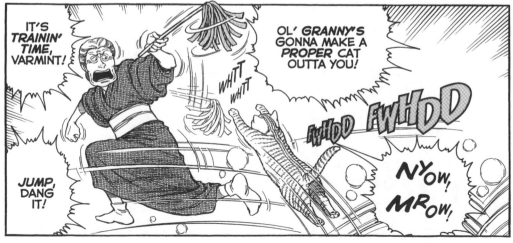

IT'S *TRAININ' TIME,* VARMINT!

JUMP, DANG IT!

OL' *GRANNY'S* GONNA MAKE A *PROPER* CAT OUTTA YOU!

WHTT WHTT

FWHDD FWHDD

NYOW, MROW!

COME ON! JUMP! AGAIN!!

NO, NO, NO!! THAT AIN'T THE WAY YUH DO IT!

WHITT WHITT

FWHDD

≶SIGHH≶ OH, GRANNY... ♥

BUT... AT LEAST NOW I CAN STEP OUT FOR AN AFTERNOON WITHOUT MICHAEL FEELING LONELY...!

HI! I'M HOME!

HMM ...?

FOLK SONGS ...?

AS IT TURNED OUT, THERE WAS ONE THING MICHAEL COULD DO THAT GRANDMA APPROVED OF... HE COULD *DANCE!*

THE END

SHOPPING

CATNIP Inc.

DIRECTOR MICHAEL...? YOUR *WIFE'S* ON LINE TWO!

OK!

HELLO, POPO?

OH, HI, DARLING. I'M *SO* SORRY TO BOTHER YOU AT WORK, BUT CAN YOU STOP BY *YUNYAR SUPERMARKET* ON YOUR WAY HOME AND PICK UP SOME THINGS?

MINI-MIKE CAUGHT COLD AND I DON'T WANT TO TAKE HIM OUTSIDE.

SURE. WHAT DO WE NEED...? OKAY... SALMON, TUNA, KITTY KIBBLES...NAIL CLIPPER BLADES AND SOME SHAMPOO. GOT IT.

OKAY, SEE YOU LATER.

KCHAK

TODAY, BUSINESSMAN MICHAEL WOULD HAVE TO DO THE SHOPPING... FOR THE FIRST TIME SINCE HE GOT MARRIED!

THIS MUST BE THE PLACE...

ユニャー ユニャー
スーパー スーパー

YUNYA

LET'S SEE... SALMON, TUNA, AND KITTY KIBBLES...

MELONS   MELONS

CARROTS

CARROTS

THERE'S NOTHING HERE BUT CARROTS AND HAY.

PRODUCE

WHERE'S THE *FISH* COUNTER ...?

THIS IS THE *UNGULATE* FLOOR, DEARIE.

FELINE SUPPLIES ARE UPSTAIRS.

OOPS... SORRY!

KAT KORNER

CANNED FOOD SALE

CHICKEN

FISH

CATNIP

KIBBLES

FINALLY! *THIS* IS THE PLACE!

WILL YOU BE NEEDING A HAND OUT, SIR?

NO, THANKS.

CASHIER

CHINGG

TODAY WE'RE HAVING A *SPECIAL PROMOTION,* SIR.

YOU CAN EXCHANGE YOUR RECEIPT FOR A CHANCE AT OUR *SPECIAL DRAWING.* FIRST PRIZE IS A TRIP TO *EUROPE* FOR THE *WHOLE FAMILY!*

REALLY...?

TROUBLE EVERY DAY

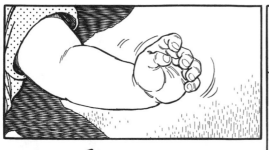

THE END

THE MAIDEN'S PRAYER

PRROWR! ♥

GEE...

WHAT'S *UP*, CATZILLA?!

YOU'RE AWFUL *LOVEY-DOVEY* THIS MORNING... DIDN'T MAMA GIVE YOU YOUR BREAKFAST?

PRRR... PRRRR

....?
....?

!?!

WHAM

: : : !!

DADDY DADDY *DADDY!*

YOU GOTTA COME QUICK!!

WHAT *NOW?*

DON'T RUN IN THE HOUSE, DEAR!

IT... IT'S...

⟩hff⟨

CATZILLA ...!!

SHE ...

SHE LEFT HALF HER FOOD!!

WHA ...?

GOOD *GOD!!*

76

Y-YOU'RE *RIGHT!* AND SHE *NEVER* LEAVES HER FOOD!

SHOULD WE CALL THE *VET?!*

MOMMA.... *WAIT!*

WHAT IF... WHAT IF... UM...

WHAT, HONEY...?

WHAT IF...

...SHE'S IN *LOVE?!*

WHAT...?!

THAT'S *INSANE!* ATE THE NEIGHBORS' *KOI,* MAYBE, BUT *LOVE?!*

DADDY! CATZILLA'S A *GIRL,* TOO!

MAYBE SHE'S *PINING* AFTER SOME CUTE *TOMCAT!*

AND SO SHE'S TOO, LIKE, *HEART-BROKEN* TO EAT!

WELL, UH...MAYBE... BUT, IF THAT'S *TRUE...WHOSE* CAT DID SHE *FALL* FOR...?

FWHAM

WHDD

SHH! AND MAKE SURE SHE DOESN'T SEE US.

'KAY, DADDY!

OH MY GOD!! THAT'S THE HOUSE OF THE *CHAIRMAN* OF THE *KUSUNOKI CORPORATION!*

AND THAT'S HIS GRAND CHAMPION AMERICAN SHORTHAIR TABBY *DAISUKE!* I HEARD HE'S WORTH *EIGHTY THOUSAND DOLLARS!!*

GIVE IT *UP,* CATZILLA!

HE'S OUT OF YOUR *CLASS!*

HAVEN'T YOU EVER LOOKED IN THE *MIRROR,* YOU SILLY CAT?!

TO BE CONTINUED...!

POOR *CATZILLA!* SHE'S TOTALLY *WASTING* AWAY.

SHE MUST JUST *ADORE* DAISUKE...!

STILL LOOKS FAT TO ME.

DADDY! CAN'T YOU ASK THEM TO LET CATZILLA *MARRY* DAISUKE?

DON'T TALK *CRAZY,* HONEY!

DAISUKE'S A *WORLD GRAND CHAMPION!*

AND EVEN *IF* THEY AGREED, THAT SNOOTY *MRS. KUSUNOKI* WOULD DEMAND *THREE THOUSAND DOLLARS* IN *STUD FEES!*

HEAR THAT? *FORGET HIM,* CATZILLA!

WHAT'S WRONG WITH THAT NICE *MICHAEL* NEXT DOOR...?

DADDYYY! SHE *HATES* MICHAEL! *HATES* HIM!

≋HFFF≋

YOWRRR!

WHOA ...?

ISN'T THAT ...?

YEAH, BABY!

QUEEN IN HEAT!!

FWHUMP

OUTTA MY WAY!!!

URK ...!

IT...IT'S CATZILLA...!

TRAPPED ...! LIKE RATS!

WH-WHAT SHOULD WE *DO?!*

IN THE *FELINE UNIVERSE,* THE *FEMALE,* NOT THE *MALE,* HAS THE RIGHT TO CHOOSE HER, ER, *MARRIAGE PARTNER.*

IN *OTHER* WORDS, HE'S GOT TO TAKE WHATEVER HE *GETS.* WE *BIOLOGISTS* HAVE A SCIENTIFIC TERM FOR THIS-- *"THE TRAGIC FATE OF ALL MEN"...!*

D-DAMN ...!

ALL RIGHT, *BOYS! I'LL* TAKE THE BULLET!

ER... MISS CATZILLA ...?

M-MARRY ME, MY DARLING!!

>Urkk!<

FWAK

PRROWR!

DADDY DADDY *DADDY!* COME *QUICK!!*

WHAT *NOW?* CALM DOWN!

IT'S CAT-ZILLA!!

D-DADDY, SHE... SHE...

SHE JUST HAD *KITTENS!*

WHA--?!

YOU'VE GOT TO BE--

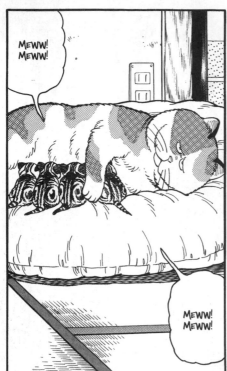

MEWW! MEWW!

MEWW! MEWW!

I *THOUGHT* SHE WAS GETTING A BIT CHUBBY... BUT IT WAS *KITTENS!*

SHE'S *ALWAYS* CHUBBY!

AND LOOK AT THESE *PATTERNS!*

TEE HEE!

MEW?

AH ...?!

GOOD FOR *YOU,* CATZILLA!

YOU MARRIED *DAISUKE!*

HOW *COULD* YOU GO OUT AND... AND *MARRY* THAT *HIDEOUS* CATZILLA?!

YOU COULD HAVE HAD *ANY* GIRL CAT YOU WANTED! *OOH!*

YES, *"THE TRAGIC FATE OF ALL MEN."* ONLY ANOTHER MAN WOULD UNDERSTAND.

THE END

86

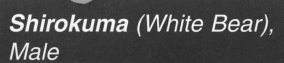

Shirokuma (White Bear), Male

Here's a pic of one of the litter of seven born between Lady and Hogan. Technically, he's the model for "Mini-Mike." Maybe because he stayed living with his mom and dad and never left home, he continues to act like a baby even after he's all grown up. Ahh...it was such a moving moment when I saw those kittens were being born! Well, to tell the truth...Lady first tried to have the delivery right by my pillow while I was having a peaceful afternoon slumber. Let me tell you, it's no way to wake up, with a yowling cat next to your ear! Anyway, I carried her out to the box I had prepared for her and she immediately started to give birth, one kitten after another, complaining like mad all the way. Shirokuma, without a care for this noble sacrifice by his mother, continues to play like a kitten at the ripe old age of eleven.

— *Makoto Kobayashi*

Dark Horse's complete line of MANGA graphic novels are available from your local comics shop or bookstore.

To find a comics shop in your area, call 1-888-266-4226

For more information or to order direct visit Darkhorse.com or call 1-800-862-0052

*Prices and availability subject to change without notice